P9-DYJ-915

The Le
Cl

Fic
Pol
c.3

Patricia Polacco

PHILOMEL BOOKS

monade
ub

Traci and Marilyn were best friends.

They were inseparable at school and almost always went to each other's houses after school. Both of them were in Miss Wichelman's fifth-grade class.

How they loved Miss Wichelman. Everyone in class did! Miss Wichelman made their classroom seem almost like home. She put a lamp on her desk, and she framed almost everyone's drawings and hung them on the walls. She had a rug right up in the front of the room next to her desk, where she read to her class from a big old rocking chair. And there was the class guinea pig, Pinky, who squeaked whenever anyone walked by him.

What everyone liked most about Miss Wichelman is that she made every kid in the classroom believe that he or she could be anything they wanted to be.

"If you dream it . . . then you can BE it!"

Marilyn wanted to be a pianist. She took lessons every week and had a grand piano in her living room. Traci loved to hear her practice.

Traci didn't know what she wanted to be, really. She did know that it made her feel warm inside whenever she was helping someone.

Almost every day, just as the last bell was about to ring, Miss Wichelman would point to a basket of fresh lemons that she always kept on her desk and say, "And if life hands you a lemon or two today—and you all know how sour lemons are—" Everyone would make a face. "Just add water and sugar and what do you have?"

Then she'd pause and the whole class would call out, "Lemonade!"

CAREER DAY
POLICEMAN
LAW ENFORCEMENT
TO SERVE AND PROTECT

Traci and Marilyn stayed after school one afternoon to help Miss Wichelman put up the Career Day posters. Miss Wichelman pinned up a picture of a doctor.

"Once I thought I'd be a doctor. Why, I even completed my pre-med courses, but I discovered being a teacher was just as important to me. After all, doctors help your bodies grow up healthy and strong, teachers help your minds grow wise and full of ideas," Miss Wichelman said thoughtfully.

Soon after, as Traci and Marilyn were walking home, they heard voices behind them. "Waddle, waddle, waddle," one of the older girls sneered.

"Fatty, fatty, two by four, couldn't get through the classroom door!" the other chimed in.

"Don't listen to them," Traci said as she pulled Marilyn along a little faster.

The older girls hissed and whispered mean secrets, then laughed as loud as they could.

Finally those mean girls turned down another street.

"I would do just about anything to be thin!" Marilyn cried.

Traci put her arm around Marilyn's shoulder.

They didn't say much more for the rest of the way home.

As weeks passed, school went on as usual, except Traci noticed that Marilyn was losing weight. She was looking great! Even the mean girls didn't tease her anymore.

Then, one Wednesday as the girls were planting flowers in Marilyn's front garden, Marilyn collapsed in a heap on the grass.

"I can't breathe," she gasped. "I'm so tired, I don't even think I can get up!"

"You haven't gone on one of those awful diets, have you, Marilyn?

Because it isn't good for kids to starve themselves and go on diets."

"That's just it," Marilyn answered. "I've lost all this weight without doing anything!"

Traci looked worried.

"It just melted off . . . but I feel so tired. And I'm always tired," Marilyn said weakly.

"I'm getting your mom." Traci knew something was very wrong.

OUR READING STARS

Marilyn didn't come back to school from that day on. Traci knew why. Marilyn's mom came over one night crying and told her mom everything. Then, the very next day, Miss Wichelman had a terrible announcement to make to the class.

"About Marilyn," Miss Wichelman started. She looked so grim that everyone in that room knew that this was something very serious. "Marilyn's family has asked me to inform all of you that Marilyn has cancer . . . leukemia."

Everyone in the room gasped. Some of the kids cried. Traci just looked at the floor and fought back her own tears.

Miss Wichelman quickly added, "But there is a great deal of hope! Marilyn will undergo a series of treatments called chemotherapy. This treatment will eventually kill all of the cancer cells in her body. But it will sometimes make her sick while it is fighting the cancer."

The whole class just sat and stared for a time.

"Is she ever coming back to school?" Danny Bridges called out.

"Yes, in a few weeks she will return, but, I warn you, she will look quite different. These treatments will make her lose all of her hair. She will probably wear a wig or a scarf, but she won't have any hair," Miss Wichelman said softly. "And there may be times that she will feel sick or very tired." Miss Wichelman suddenly lost all of the color in her face and quickly sat down.

"But Miss Wichelman, people die when they get cancer, don't they?" one of the children blurted out.

Miss Wichelman stared out the window for a moment, then collected herself. "There is no doubt that some do not survive. Our Marilyn most certainly will, but she'll need all of us to help her through this!"

Traci stared at the basket of lemons and thought to herself that no matter how much sugar was added, there wasn't going to be lemonade this time.

As days passed, Traci and Miss Wichelman were almost permanent fixtures at Marilyn's house.

One day, shortly after her chemo began, Traci walked in while Marilyn was brushing her hair. She was staring at her hairbrush—it was full of strands and clumps of her beautiful hair!

"My hair . . . it's falling out!" Marilyn cried as she pulled the hair from the brush and tried to put it back on her head. "I even made a wish on a star last night that I wouldn't lose my hair!" Marilyn sobbed.

From that day on, some days were good and some weren't for Marilyn.

Get Well
Marilyn

One day, Miss Wichelman came for a visit. Traci was already there. It was one of Marilyn's not-so-good days. She had just come from the hospital, and her arms were bruised from all the pokes she got that day. She was so weak, she could hardly sit up in bed. Nothing Traci and Miss Wichelman did seemed to cheer her up.

"Look, Marilyn, Miss Wichelman brought you a CD of a piano concerto to listen to . . . Mozart—your favorite composer."

"Music! I don't care about music. I'm never going to be able to play the piano again with these sore arms. I'm so sick of doctors and hospitals and needles."

"Oh, Marilyn, please smile. Smile just for me," Traci pleaded.

Marilyn cried even more. "Smile? How can I smile? I feel so sick! No one knows how bad I feel. NO ONE!" Then she buried her head in her pillow.

Miss Wichelman held Marilyn in her arms. "Oh, sweet pea, I think I do. I think I know exactly how you feel," Miss Wichelman said softly. Then Miss Wichelman sat back and held Marilyn's face in her hands.

"Marilyn, you just have to get well . . . so you can come to my wedding!" Miss Wichelman beamed.

"Your wedding!" Marilyn and Traci both called out.

"When did you get engaged . . . and to who?" Marilyn smiled broadly for the first time in weeks.

"His name is Warren—and, girls, this will have to be our secret for a while. But I want you both to be there. I want you both in yellow dresses. Lemon yellow as bright as sunshine. We're going to make lemonade out of sour, bitter old lemons, aren't we," Miss Wichelman whispered.

"But what if I'm still bald? What then?" Marilyn asked.

"Well . . . so what! What if you are? You'll still be one of the most beautiful girls there," Miss Wichelman reassured her.

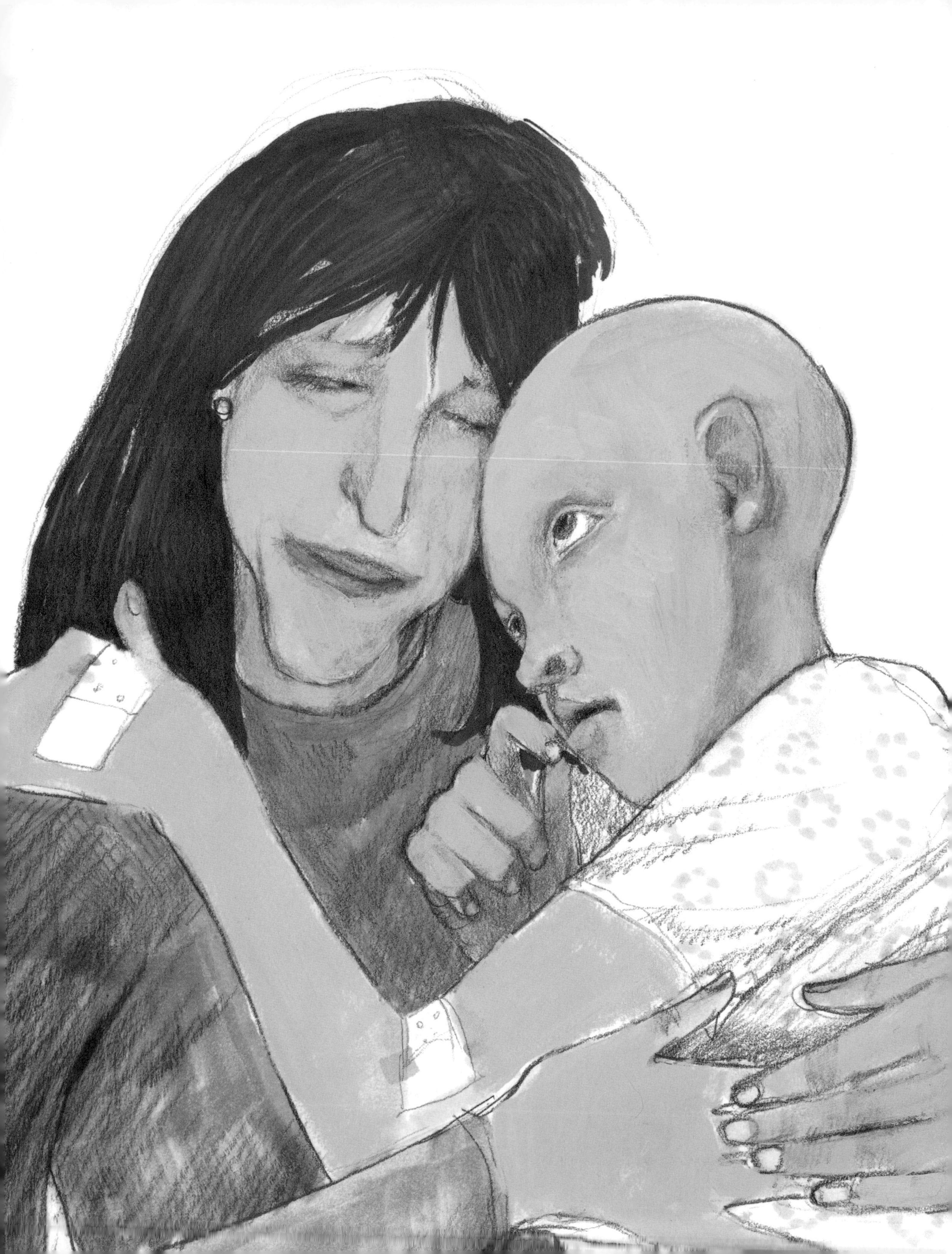

It was Monday morning. Miss Wichelman and Traci and the whole class had a huge surprise for Marilyn's return to school. It had been planned that Marilyn be brought to class just after the starting bell so the kids could get their surprise ready. As Marilyn walked down the hall, she was gripping her mother's hand. She had on her best scarf.

Traci opened the door and greeted her. The whole class stood up. They were all wearing funny hats.

As Marilyn entered, everyone cheered and clapped. There was a big sheet cake on Miss Wichelman's desk. Traci took Marilyn's hands. "Welcome back, Marilyn!" she called out.

Then she pulled off her funny hat. Everyone in class did.

Everyone was bald!

They had all shaved their heads.

Marilyn's mother caught her breath and clapped her hand over her mouth. Marilyn walked up and down each aisle, looking intently into the face of each of her classmates.

Welcome Back
Marily
we miss
you!

When she passed the last desk, she lowered her eyes and slowly pulled off her own scarf and held it in her hands. She felt a warm hand softly caress her hairless head. It was Miss Wichelman.

Then everyone gasped. "Look!"

Miss Wichelman slowly pulled off her own brightly colored scarf.

She too had no hair.

Then there was a loud cheer, the music was turned on, ice cream and cake dished out, and the celebration began!

But Miss Wichelman seemed distracted. She didn't seem as cheerful as usual.

With each treatment the doctor said Marilyn's cancer was disappearing. Marilyn finally completed her last round of chemo. Her hair started growing back right away. It was fuzzy and orange at first, but soon it looked just like it had before, except it was curly and shorter.

She and Traci met after school under the shady elm with Miss Wichelman every week. They had become very close. They called themselves "The Lemonade Club." Miss Wichelman read poems. Sometimes she cried. She said it was "because the words are so beautiful."

They talked about everything! And, of course, they loved hearing about plans for Miss Wichelman's wedding.

Soon the entire class returned to a normal routine. Everyone's hair was growing back. But, one day, Bernie Carlisle called out, "Hey, Miss Wichelman, how come you're still wearing your scarf? Ain't you got no hair under there?" Although Miss Wichelman knew he was kidding, she didn't laugh. She tugged at her scarf and looked out the window. Something seemed wrong.

Traci passed a note to Miss Wichelman that read, "Emergency meeting of the Lemonade Club today after school under the elm!"

LEMONADE CLUB
TODAY!
AFTER

Later that day Traci and Marilyn sat under the shade of the old elm tree. It was Marilyn who spoke up. "You have it, too, don't you, Miss Wichelman . . . for real. That's why you said you knew exactly how I felt!"

Miss Wichelman couldn't seem to speak, and when she finally did, her eyes filled with tears. "I have breast cancer, girls," she said, almost in a whisper.

"So you're going to fight this, aren't you?" Marilyn demanded.

"Yes, I'm almost finished with chemo. . . ." Miss Wichelman said as her voice trailed off.

"Will that get rid of it?" Traci asked.

"No, I'll have to have surgery eventually," Miss Wichelman answered.

"Surgery! I didn't have surgery!" Marilyn said.

"You had cancer in a very different way than I do."

"So . . . so you're going to be flat-chested like us, right?" Traci chirped. "Way to go, Miss Wichelman!" she added, giving a thumbs-up.

"Fashion models are flat-chested, and they are considered the most beautiful women on earth!" Marilyn chimed in.

"Except for brides!" said Traci.

Then they all laughed.

Miss Wichelman seemed deep in thought.

"I don't know what I would do without you two." Miss Wichelman sighed as she lay back on the grass and looked at the clouds.

"Both of you have taught me so much and affected my life. Because of you, I have thought again about being a doctor. I applied to Stanford Medical School . . . I wanted to help children just like you, Marilyn. But since I started the treatments, I think I have lost my courage." Miss Wichelman's voice drifted off.

"Hey!" Marilyn bellowed. "You aren't going to let something like cancer stomp on your dreams, are you?"

"You are always teaching us to keep our dreams, no matter what!" Traci added.

"If you can dream it, you can BE it," the three of them said together.

"You'll make a wonderful doctor," Traci whispered.
"And Warren loves you. What more could you want?" Marilyn said.
Miss Wichelman took a lemon out of her basket.
"Well, then, girls . . . to the Lemonade Club!" she said triumphantly.
"To the Lemonade Club," Traci and Marilyn echoed.

It was an especially sunny day. People were gathering in the church. Even though it had been five years since they had been Miss Wichelman's students, almost the whole class from then was sitting together. The music was playing softly. It was one of Miss Wichelman's favorite hymns. The flowers were so beautiful. Everyone there was thinking about Miss Wichelman.

Suddenly the congregation sprang to its feet. The music boomed a joyous trumpet voluntary . . . and there standing in their lemon yellow gowns were Traci and Marilyn. They beamed as they marched down the aisle to join the groom at the front of the church.

Then everyone turned and looked as Cynthia Wichelman appeared. Traci and Marilyn were right; she was a beautiful bride. She glowed as she floated like a cloud down the aisle. Dr. Cynthia Wichelman became the wife of Dr. Warren Gish on this glorious day! And they were all there together to celebrate it. A sweet lemonade, indeed.

Cynthia and Warren

Traci (right) and Marilyn (left)

Cynthia and Patricia Polacco

As for the Lemonade Club, the three friends—Traci, Marilyn, and Miss Wichelman—still keep in touch to this very day. Traci went on to study in the medical field, inspired by Miss Wichelman. Marilyn became a teacher who is deeply loved, just like Miss Wichelman always was. Marilyn has three sons now and still plays the piano. Cynthia and Warren live in Missouri, where Cynthia teaches medical studies and Warren is a tireless researcher dedicated to finding cures for disease.

* * *

I know all of this to be true because Traci is my daughter. And Marilyn is one of her best friends, and Cynthia is, indeed, my daughter's former teacher who went on to become a doctor after battling cancer and winning. She is very dear to my entire family, for we look to her and her example to find our own courage, inspiration and most of all . . . hope.

For Marilyn, Traci, Diane, and Cynthia for her dedication to her students, and her remarkable courage.

Patricia Lee Gauch, Editor

PHILOMEL BOOKS
A division of Penguin Young Readers Group.
Published by The Penguin Group.
Penguin Group (USA) Inc., 375 Hudson Street, New York, NY 10014, U.S.A.
Penguin Group (Canada), 90 Eglinton Avenue East, Suite 700, Toronto, Ontario, Canada M4P 2Y3
(a division of Pearson Penguin Canada Inc.).
Penguin Books Ltd, 80 Strand, London WC2R 0RL, England.
Penguin Ireland, 25 St. Stephen's Green, Dublin 2, Ireland (a division of Penguin Books Ltd.).
Penguin Group (Australia), 250 Camberwell Road, Camberwell, Victoria 3124, Australia (a division of Pearson Australia Group Pty Ltd).
Penguin Books India Pvt Ltd, 11 Community Centre, Panchsheel Park, New Delhi - 110 017, India.
Penguin Group (NZ), 67 Apollo Drive, Rosedale, North Shore 0745, Auckland, New Zealand
(a division of Pearson New Zealand Ltd).
Penguin Books (South Africa) (Pty) Ltd, 24 Sturdee Avenue, Rosebank, Johannesburg 2196, South Africa.
Penguin Books Ltd, Registered Offices: 80 Strand, London WC2R 0RL, England.

Copyright © 2007 by Babushka Inc.

All rights reserved. This book, or parts thereof, may not be reproduced in any form without permission in writing from the publisher, Philomel Books, a division of Penguin Young Readers Group, 345 Hudson Street, New York, NY 10014. Philomel Books, Reg. U.S. Pat. & Tm. Off. The scanning, uploading and distribution of this book via the Internet or via any other means without the permission of the publisher is illegal and punishable by law. Please purchase only authorized electronic editions, and do not participate in or encourage electronic piracy of copyrighted materials. Your support of the author's rights is appreciated. The publisher does not have any control over and does not assume any responsibility for author or third-party websites or their content.
Published simultaneously in Canada. Manufactured in China by South China Printing Co. Ltd.
Design by Semadar Megged. Text set in 16-point Adobe Jenson.
The illustrations are rendered in pencils and markers.
Library of Congress Cataloging-in-Publication Data

ISBN 978-0-399-24540-4
1 3 5 7 9 10 8 6 4 2
First Impression

38 McElwain Street
Merrimack, NH 03054